One of a Kind

For Jason, one of a kind —D. H.

ALADDIN

An imprint of Simon & Schuster Children's Publishing Division

1230 Avenue of the Americas, New York, NY 10020

First Aladdin hardcover edition June 2012

Text copyright © 2012 by Ariel S. Winter

Illustrations copyright © 2012 by David Hitch

ALADDIN is a trademark of Simon & Schuster, Inc., and related logo

is a registered trademark of Simon & Schuster, Inc.

For information about special discounts for bulk purchases,

please contact Simon & Schuster Special Sales at 1-866-506-1949 or business@simonandschuster.com.

The Simon & Schuster Speakers Bureau can bring authors to your live event.

For more information or to book an event contact the Simon & Schuster Speakers Bureau

at 1-866-248-3049 or visit our website at www.simonspeakers.com.

Designed by Karin Paprocki

The text of this book was set in Colwell Roman.

Manufactured in China 0312 SCP

2 4 6 8 10 9 7 5 3 1

Library of Congress Cataloging-in-Publication Data

Winter, Ariel S.

One of a Kind / by Ariel S. Winter ; illustrated by David Hitch.

1st Aladdin hardcover ed. p. cm.

Summary: Lysander Singleton tries his best to fit in at Twin Oaks Elementary,

where all students are twins except him, but on the day of the Twindividuation contest

his experience as an only child gives him a competitive edge.

ISBN 978-1-4424-2016-8 (hardcover)

ISBN 978-1-4424-5308-1 (eBook)

1. Only child–Fiction. 2. Twins–Fiction. 3. Brothers and sisters–Fiction.

4. Individuality–Fiction. 5. Schools–Fiction. I. Hitch, David, ill. II. Title.

PZ7.W754Lys 2012 / [E]–dc22 / 2010043538

One of a Kind

Aladdin

NEW YORK LONDON TORONTO SYDNEY NEW DELHI

Lysander Singleton was the only *only* child at Twin Oaks Elementary.

At first,
he tried to fit in.

On occasion the other children would let him play at recess.

But the only classmates who would be his friends were also unpopular. This left Lysander feeling rather unimportant.

Every year, Twin Oaks Elementary held a series of events meant to encourage individuality known as the Twindividuation.

At the start of the daylong competition, the twins were divided into two separate teams.

And given uniforms,
none of which matched.

With no sibling to be individuated
from, and his general sense that
he would always be alone,
Lysander expected to be left out.

For some reason, however, he found himself to be much in demand.

Once it was decided
he would play for both
teams alternately,
the games got underway
with a trust fall.

The children met with mixed results, but Lysander, practiced at distrust and uncertainty, wasn't falling for anything.

At the choral performance, twin after twin struggled through solo renditions of their practiced two-part harmonies, while Lysander timidly managed a melody entirely on his own.

His success started to garner some positive attention.

With growing confidence, Lysander tackled the
written part of the competition, which seemed
so easy he wondered if he was doing it right.

*Describe what makes you
unique from any other person.
(Including your siblings.)*

List your favorite activities.

*When you are alone in a
forest, do you hear any
sounds?*

Next it was time for the Isolated Ice Cream Inquiry, in which the children each chose from forty-five flavors without the benefit of sibling consultation, and were scored on how long it took them to reach a decision.

Lysander, with something bordering
on self-assurance, chose Monkey Butter
Chocolate Chip in a record setting
fifteen seconds.

During the one-man relay,
Lysander sailed ahead with poise
as his classmates watched in awe.

When their disastrous turns came,
Lysander made a show of good
sportsmanship with polite applause.

At the end of the day,
the teachers tallied
the scores. . . .

Scores

Lysander 100

Kara 50   Leda 12

Elvis 21   Paul

Casey 10   Clark 22

Leah 19   Leda 50

Lysander came in first in every event. Since he had played for both teams, the Twindividuation ended in a tie.

The entire school
rushed at him. . . .

And raised him
in triumph.

Lysander was presented with the Simondon-Stiegler Cup, the individual award for individuality. He felt very important.

Practically a hero,
Lysander enjoyed his due rewards.

Lysander Singleton
was the *only* only child at
Twin Oaks Elementary.